P9-EML-404

IF I FOUND A
WISTFUL UNICORN

To Martin

Published by
PEACHTREE PUBLISHERS, LTD.
494 Armour Circle, NE
Atlanta, Georgia 30324

Text © 1978 by Ann Ashford
Illustrations © 1978 by Wilfred H. Drath

All rights reserved.

Manufactured in the United States of America

First Printing (1992)

ISBN: 1-56145-047-2
Library of Congress Catalog Card Number 78-59094

IF I FOUND A WISTFUL UNICORN

Ann Ashford

Illustrations by Bill Drath

PEACHTREE PUBLISHERS, LTD.
Atlanta

IF I FOUND A WISTFUL UNICORN
AND BROUGHT HIM TO YOU, ALL FORLORN···
WOULD YOU PET HIM ?

IF I TOOK AN EMPTY MIDNIGHT TRAIN

ACROSS THE COUNTRY IN THE RAIN...

WOULD YOU MEET ME ?

IF I PICKED A LITTLE FLOWER UP
AND PUT IT IN A PAPER CUP...

WOULD YOU SMELL IT ?

IF I FOUND A SECRET PLACE TO GO,

WITH YOU THE ONLY ONE TO KNOW ...

WOULD YOU BE THERE ?

IF MY CRICKET COUGHED AND GOT THE FLU

AND NEEDED WARMTH AND COMFORT TOO...

WOULD YOU HOLD HIM ?

IF MY RAINBOW WERE TO TURN ALL GRAY
AND WOULDN'T SHINE AT ALL TODAY ...

IF MY SOUL WERE FEELING ALL ALONE
AND WASN'T NEAR A TELEPHONE...

WOULD YOU BRING ONE ?

IF MY BIRCH TREE WERE AFRAID AT NIGHT
AND COULDN'T SLEEP WITHOUT A LIGHT---

WOULD YOU PAINT IT ?

WOULD YOU WRITE TO IT ?

IF MY CLOCK DEVELOPED NERVOUS STRAIN

TICK   TICK   TICK

AND NEEDED HELP TO "TOCK" AGAIN ...

WOULD YOU FIX IT ?

IF I RAN BACKWARDS UP A TREE

AND CALLED FOR YOU TO

IF MY TURTLE GOT A NERVOUS TIC
AND COULDN'T SWIM 'CAUSE HE WAS SICK...

IF I SAID THAT I COULD DANCE FOR YOU
AS HARD AS THAT WOULD BE TO DO ···

WOULD YOU WATCH ME ?

AND BIT ME FIERCELY ON THE KNEE ...

WOULD YOU BANDAGE IT ?

IF MY OBELISK CAME TUMBLING DOWN
AND FELL IN PIECES ON THE GROUND...

WOULD YOU PICK IT UP ?

IF MY NIGHTINGALE WERE A MONOTONE

AND MUCH TOO SHY TO SING ALONE ...

WOULD YOU HUM WITH HIM ?

IF MY WART DECIDED YESTERDAY

TO BE A DIMPLE ANYWAY ...

WOULD YOU NOTICE ?

IF ALL THAT I WOULD WANT TO DO

WOULD BE TO SIT AND TALK TO YOU...

WOULD YOU LISTEN ?

IF ANY OF THESE THINGS YOU'LL DO,

I'LL NEVER HAVE TO SAY TO YOU...

"DO YOU LOVE ME ?"

ANN ASHFORD
author

Ann Ashford was born in 1939 in Hannibal, Missouri,
and raised on the Upper Peninsula of Michigan.
She graduated from Agnes Scott College in 1961
and was a United Methodist church worker for migrants
in Texas, a welfare case worker in Atlanta, a teacher,
an actress, and vice-president of a family-owned
fund-raising consulting firm.
IF I FOUND A WISTFUL UNICORN was the first book
published by Peachtree Publishers, Ltd. It won the
Award for Juvenile Literature from the Council of Authors
and Journalists. Ann Ashford died in 1988.

BILL DRATH
illustrator

Bill Drath was born in 1915 in Wisconsin. A graduate
of the University of Wisconsin, he served in the Army
during World War II (earning a Bronze Star) and
the Korean War, retiring in 1966 as a lieutenant
colonel. In addition to WISTFUL UNICORN, Drath also
illustrated WILLOWCAT AND THE CHIMNEY SWEEP and
SOUTHERN IS.... He died in 1991.